Welcome to the Forest, where
THE MINISTRY OF MONSTERS
helps humans and monsters live side
by side in peace and harmony...

CONNOR O'GOYLE
lives here too, with his gargoyle mum,
human dad and his dog, Trixie.
But Connor's no ordinary boy...

When monsters get out of control,
Connor's the one for the job.
He's half-monster, he's the Ministry's
NUMBER ONE AGENT,
and he's licensed to do things
no one else can do. He's...

MONSTER BOY!

For Millie Collins, Reece Mansfield,
Abbie O'Connell and Ben Rees,
My forgotten marketeers!

First published in 2009 by Orchard Books
First paperback publication in 2010

ORCHARD BOOKS
338 Euston Road, London NW1 3BH
Orchard Books Australia
Level 17/207 Kent St, Sydney, NSW 2000

ISBN 978 1 40830 240 8 (hardback)
ISBN 978 1 40830 248 4 (paperback)

Text and illustrations © Shoo Rayner 2009

The right of Shoo Rayner to be identified as the author and
illustrator of this work has been asserted by him in accordance with the
Copyright, Designs and Patents Act, 1988.

A CIP catalogue record for this book is available from the British Library.

1 3 5 7 9 10 8 6 4 2 (hardback)
1 3 5 7 9 10 8 6 4 2 (paperback)

Printed in Great Britain

Orchard Books is a division of Hachette Children's Books,
an Hachette UK company.

www.hachette.co.uk

MONSTER BOY

DINO DESTROYER

SHOO RAYNER

ORCHARD BOOKS

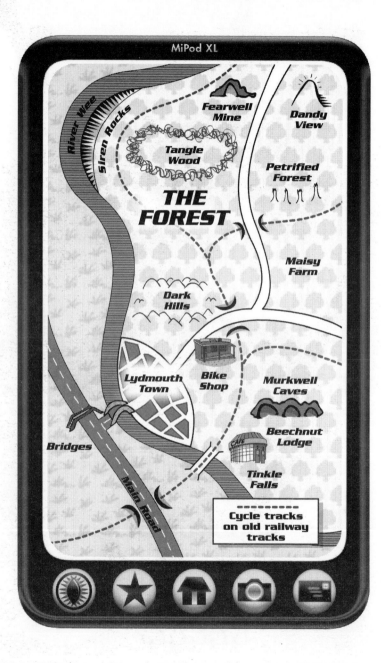

"Go fetch, girl!" Connor yelled, throwing a stick high into the air.

Trixie unfurled her wings
and zoomed after the stick.
As she snapped at it, her
wings stopped beating. She
froze in midair. Something
had scared her.

Her eyes opened
wide and her fur
stood up on end.
The stick tumbled
to the ground.

"You missed!"
Connor teased
his dog.

Trixie yelped and dropped like a brick. She fell into Connor's arms, knocking him flat on the ground.

"*Oof!* W-w-what the...?" Connor stammered.

A monstrous shape loomed against the skyline. A giant, scaly leg with dagger-sharp claws smashed into the ground, exactly where Connor had been standing a few seconds before.

BOOM!

The huge, deadly dinosaur lurched past him, tearing a path through the Forest as it headed off towards the town.

Trixie licked Connor's face and wagged her tail.

"Hey, stop it!" Connor complained. Then he looked into his faithful friend's eyes. "Thanks, Trix. I think you just saved my life!"

An emergency alarm went off in Connor's pocket. He pulled out his MiPod and read the screen.

MiPod XL

MISSION ALERT!

To: Monster Boy,
Number One Agent

From: Mission Control,
Ministry of Monsters

Subject: Emergency in
Beechnut Woods

Dinosaur (Tyrannosaurus Rex) on the
rampage. Please investigate immediately.

Dinosaurs can be dangerous.
Approach with care.

Good luck!

M.O.M.

THIS MESSAGE WILL
SELF-ERASE IN
FIFTEEN SECONDS

Connor raced into the
Pedal-O bike hire shop
where he lived with his
mum and dad.

Mum looked up from the
mountain bike she was fixing.
"What's up?" she asked calmly.
She was used to Connor's
monster emergencies.

"I need MB3, and fast," said Connor.

Mum wheeled the gleaming bike out of the secret store.

"I've put some sandwiches and a bottle of water in the back," she told Connor. "Now be careful, wear your helmet, and give your mum a kiss before you go!"

"Oh, *Mum!*"

Connor's mum was a Gargoyle, so
Connor was half-monster. His code-name
was Monster Boy. If anyone could look
after himself, Connor could.

Connor raced off down the old railway track that was now a forest bike path. Trixie leant out of her basket on the handlebars. She loved to feel the wind in her ears.

They were soon in town, looking for signs of the dinosaur.

"Wuff!" Trixie pointed her nose towards a terrifying scene of devastation.

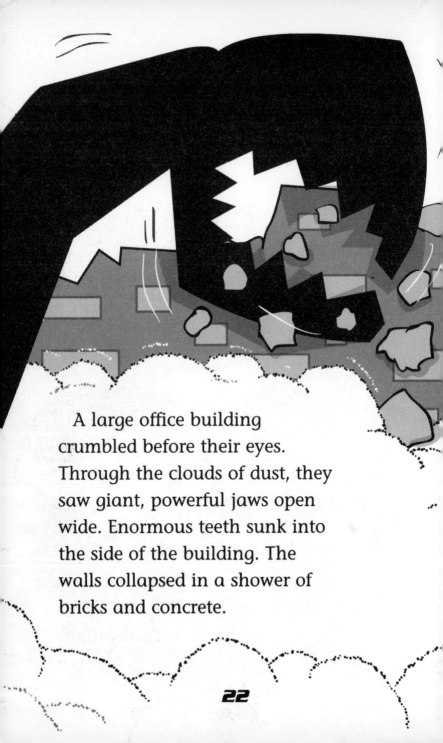

A large office building
crumbled before their eyes.
Through the clouds of dust, they
saw giant, powerful jaws open
wide. Enormous teeth sunk into
the side of the building. The
walls collapsed in a shower of
bricks and concrete.

"Excuse me!" Connor called out to a man in a bright yellow builder's helmet. "Have you seen a dinosaur round here?"

"No dinosaurs here, mate," the man called back. "Only that old monster there." He pointed to the demolition machine that soared high above them. Its mechanical jaws tore into the building, biting out the window frames and chomping up the roof tiles.

Something was written on the machine's long, extending arm. Connor screwed up his eyes. "Raze-It Demolition Corporation," he read aloud.

"Aye," said the man. "That's us. Now, you'd better move along. It's dangerous round here."

MiPOD MONSTER IDENTIFIER PROGRAM

Monster:

Tyrannosaurus Rex

Distinguishing Features:
Sharp teeth and claws.

Preferred Habitat:
Pre-historic Earth.

Essential Information:
A few dinosaurs survive in the Forest. Sadly, there is only one Tyrannosaurus Rex left. He is happy as long as he lets off steam once in a while, but he often gets bored and lonely.

Danger Rating: 5

On the footbridge over the main road, Connor saw what he had most feared. The dinosaur roared as cars skidded and crashed into each other. Frightened drivers and passengers ran for their lives.

"T-Rex, stop!" Connor shouted.

The huge beast turned its giant head and glared at him. It picked up an abandoned car and ripped it in half with its teeth. "You gonna make me?" T-Rex roared.

T-Rex clawed open the side of a truck and scrunched up a bus as if it were made of cardboard. In no time the road looked like a scrap yard.

Connor had to stop T-Rex before he did more damage. But how?

Connor's MiPod pinged again. It was a message from his dad, Gary O'Goyle, the world-famous Mountain Bike Champion. Dad always sent messages at the most unhelpful times!

HOLLYWOOD

Hi son,

Having a great time at the Hollywood Celebrity Mountain Bike Race. Here's a picture of me and Cowboy Jim, the rodeo star – I got his autograph for you!

Lots of love,
Dad

"Cowboy Jim!" Connor whooped. "That gives me an idea. Thanks, Dad!"

"Ready?" Connor asked his faithful pet. Trixie wagged her tail and snuffed her nose in a sneeze of joy. She loved chasing monsters!

32

Connor aimed the bike's handlebars at the dinosaur's legs. He flipped open the lid of his bell and pressed the red launch button. "Fire!"

Two missiles streaked out of the front suspension forks. Each missile spun a fine thread behind it. The thread was a top-secret material. Made from a giant monster spider's web, it was ten times stronger than steel, but felt as soft as silk.

MONSTER BIKE INFO

MB3

MB3 is a capture bike. It has many attachments to suit different monsters.

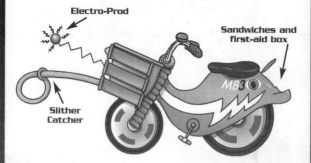

MB3 Monster Missiles are radio-controlled from the handlebars.

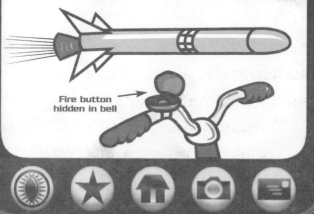

Connor guided the missiles using the handlebars as controllers.

The missiles wrapped the thread round and round T-Rex's legs.

Trixie knew what to do. She flew
around the dinosaur's head to distract
him. He snapped his powerful jaws
and lunged at her. The thread wound
tighter and tighter around his legs.

One final snap at the brave little dog made the lumbering beast lose his balance. T-Rex came crashing to the ground.

Soon the monster lay silent and helpless in the middle of the road.

Connor patted his happy, tail-wagging friend. "Nice work, Trix!"

Connor stood over the
monster and stared into
its giant yellow eyes.

"Now, have you quite
finished, T-Rex?"
Connor sighed.

The dinosaur snorted and slumped his huge head on the ground – defeated by a boy and his dog!

But Connor was half-monster himself. He understood that monsters have feelings too.

"You can't go around eating cars whenever you feel like it," Connor whispered to the beast.

"But...I've got an
idea you might just
be interested in!"

"So where's T-Rex now?" asked Connor's mum as they cycled into town to do the weekly shop.

"You'll see in a minute," Connor told her, with a twinkle in his eye.

Mum knew that he had come up with one of his monster solutions. Connor liked to help monsters with their problems.

Connor's brakes squealed. "There!" he said, pointing at the demolition site.

T-Rex and the enormous wrecking machine moved together in a dance of destruction. Together they ripped and slashed and chomped and bashed their way through the office building. It was almost beautiful to watch.

The man in the
yellow helmet came
up and shook
Connor's hand.
"T-Rex is the best
worker we've ever
had," he laughed.

"They look so happy together," Mum said, as she watched the dinosaur and the wrecking machine work together in perfect harmony.

Connor smiled. "Poor old T-Rex – all he needed was someone like him to play with!"

"Wuff!" Trixie had found a piece of wood. She dropped it at Connor's feet.

Connor laughed. "Want to play too, Trix?" He picked up the stick and threw it high into the sky. "Go fetch, girl!"

SHOO RAYNER
MONSTER BOY

All priced at £3.99

The Monster Boy stories are available from all good bookshops,
or can be ordered direct from the publisher:
Orchard Books, PO BOX 29, Douglas IM99 1BQ
Credit card orders please telephone 01624 836000
or fax 01624 837033 or visit our website: www.orchardbooks.co.uk
or e-mail: bookshop@enterprise.net for details.

To order please quote title, author and ISBN
and your full name and address.
Cheques and postal orders should be made payable to 'Bookpost plc.'
Postage and packing is FREE within the UK
(overseas customers should add £2.00 per book).

Prices and availability are subject to change.